LEARN
with
THOMAS

CHRISTOPHER AWDRY • KEN STOTT

Random House 🏠 New York

ENGINES

Duck

Gordon

Edward

James

Toby

Can you name the engines?

Which is the biggest engine?

Which engines
are twins?

Which one is
your favorite?

How many
engines are blue?

Henry

Douglas

Percy

Donald

Thomas

hippopotamus

tiger

giraffe

lion

panda

ZOO

This animal likes wallowing in the mud. What is its name?

What is the striped animal
Thomas can see in the shed?

What tall animal
is James carrying?

This is the king of the
jungle. What animal is it?

What animal likes to
eat bamboo shoots?

What's that animal sitting on Bertie's radiator?

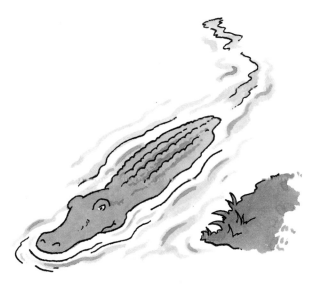

Who's hiding in the water?

This bird likes ice and snow.

Henry found this animal in his tunnel. What is it?

This animal likes climbing trees.

monkey

crocodile

penguin

elephant

bear

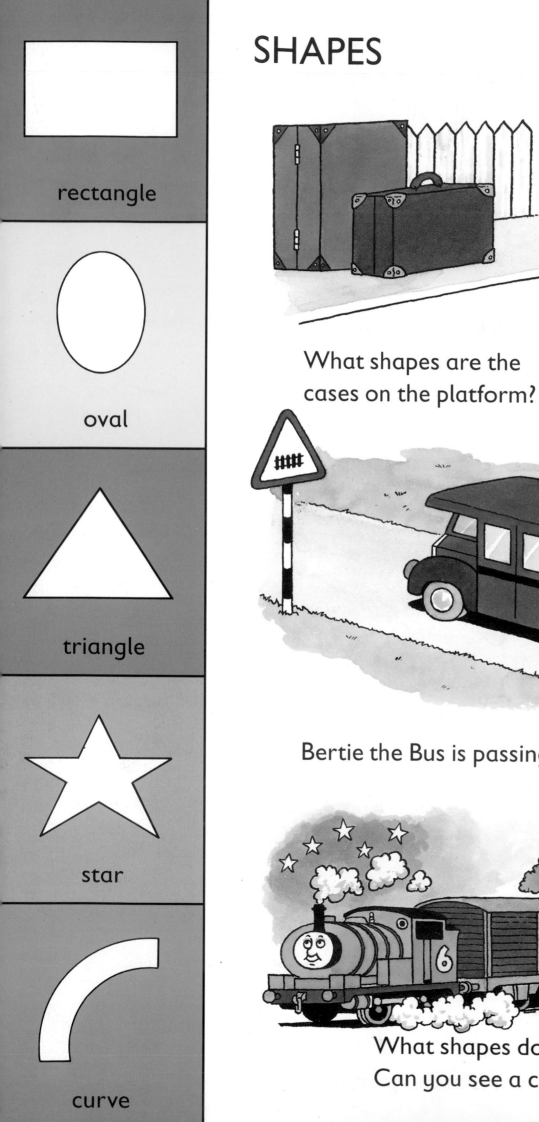

SHAPES

rectangle	
oval	
triangle	
star	
curve	

What shapes are the cases on the platform?

What shape is the picture of Sir Topham Hatt and his wife?

Bertie the Bus is passing a road sign. What shape is it?

What shapes does Percy see in the sky?
Can you see a curve in this picture?

Thomas's wheels are round like a circle. How many other circles can you see?

Sir Topham is waving from his window. What shape is the window?

What shape is the station flower bed?

Can you see Toby's bell?

Thomas loves his coaches, Annie and Clarabel, with all his heart. Count the hearts in this picture.

circle

square

diamond

bell

heart

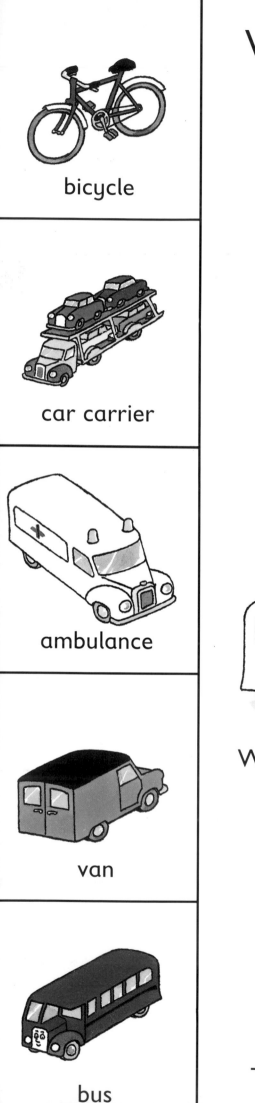

bicycle

car carrier

ambulance

van

bus

WHEELS

How many bicycles are left at the station?

The car carrier takes cars to the showroom.

What kind of vehicle is this?

Whom does this van belong to?

Thomas is having a race with Bertie the Bus. Who is winning?

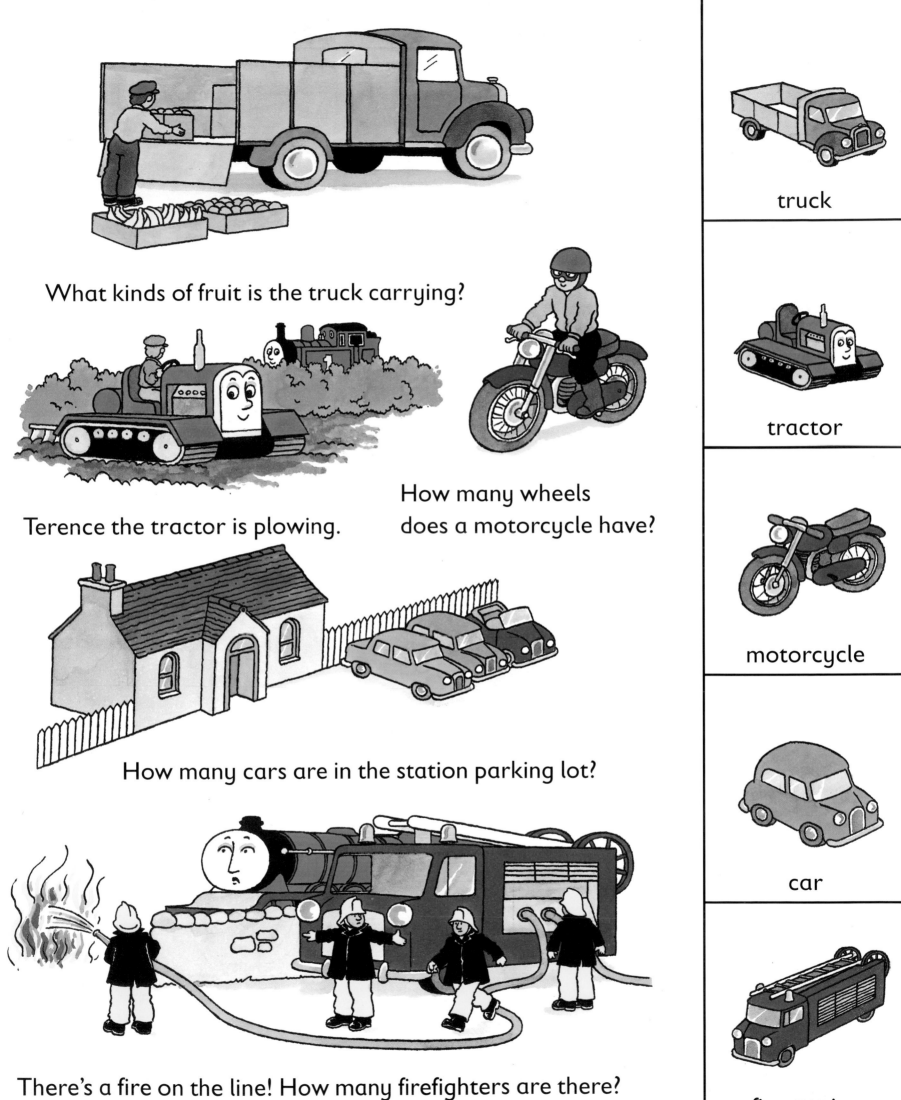

What kinds of fruit is the truck carrying?

Terence the tractor is plowing.

How many wheels does a motorcycle have?

How many cars are in the station parking lot?

There's a fire on the line! How many firefighters are there?

truck

tractor

motorcycle

car

fire engine

STATION

tickets

headlamp

whistle

schedule

case

The ticket collector checks the tickets.

What color is James? What color is his headlamp?

KNAPFORD	ELSBRIDGE
6·00 · 6·30	7·10 · 7·40
7·00 · 7·30	8·10 · 8·40
8·00 · 8·30	9·10 · 9·40
9·00 · 9·30	10·10 · 10·40
10·00 · 10·30	11·10 · 11·40
11·00 · 11·30	12·10 · 12·40

VICARSTOWN	ARLESBURGH
6·00 · 6·30	7·10 · 7·40
7·00 · 7·30	8·40
8·00 · 8·30	9·40
9·00 · 9·30	10·40
10·00 · 10·30	11·40
11·00 · 11·30	12·40

Who blows the whistle? How many cases are on the platform?

What is Sir Topham Hatt looking at?

Which engine is pulling the train?

Can you see the driver? Who goes with him in the cab? Is it the fireman?

Where does the conductor ride?

What shape are the buffers?

engine

train

conductor

driver

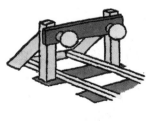

buffers

NUMBERS

1 one	
2 two	
3 three	
4 four	
5 five	

Here is one engine.
Do you know his name?

How many cranes
are lifting Henry?

How many freight cars is Percy pulling?

How many cats does
Sir Topham have?

How many umbrellas
has the conductor found?

James will pull the circus train. How many monkeys are in the car?

How many mailbags are sitting on the platform?

How many chickens do you see?

Can you count the people on the platform?

How many pieces of cake has the driver cut?

6 six

7 seven

8 eight

9 nine

10 ten

SEASIDE

fish

seashells

sea

sandcastles

lighthouse

What is in the rock pool?

Count the seashells.

What is swimming with the two children in the sea?
How many sandcastles are there?

The lighthouse signals to the ships at night,
warning them to stay clear of the rocks.

Percy is collecting wood from the cargo ship.

How many people are waiting on the wharf for a boat trip?

The helicopter flies over the beach to make sure people are safe in the water.

What colors are the yachts?

Sometimes people fish from the end of the pier.
How many fishing rods can you count?

ship

helicopter

wharf

yacht

pier

COLORS

James is a red engine. What color is his dome?

Percy is green. What color stripes does he have?

Do you know what color Terence the tractor is?

This is Toby the Tram Engine. What color is he?

Thomas is arriving to pick up some passengers. Where is the lady with the pink hat?

Thomas the Tank
Engine is blue.
What other colors
is he painted?

This is Edward.
What color is he?

Sir Topham Hatt is
wearing a black jacket.
What color is his vest?

Sir Topham Hatt's wife has
an umbrella. What color is it?

Harold is white.
What color are his stripes?

yellow

blue

black

purple

white

WEATHER

rainbow

wind

ice

snow

gale

When the sun comes out after the rain, what does Percy see in the sky?

What has happened to Sir Topham's hat?

James wonders why the ducks are sliding. What has happened to the pond?

Thomas is stuck in the snowdrift. What color is the snow?

What made this tree fall on the line?

On sunny days, Thomas takes children to the seaside. How many children can you see?

Thunder rumbles and lightning flashes. Toby is out in a storm.

Why can't Percy see Harold the Helicopter?

Why is Henry staying in the tunnel?

Why is Gordon traveling slowly today?

sun

storm

clouds

rain

fog

cat

chicken

sheep

farmer

dog

FARM

Can you find the cat?
Where is it sleeping?

Some chickens have got into
the railway yard. How many
are left in the farmyard?

A sheep with a gray face is missing. The shepherd cannot
see it. Can you?

Henry can see the farm dog.
Can he see the farmer? Where is he?

The scarecrow frightens away the birds. How many birds can you see?

What kind of farm machine is Terence?

Who lives in the stable?

How many pigs are here? How many goats?

James is watching the cows. How many can you see?

scarecrow

tractor

horse

pig

cow

over

up

open

wide

big

OPPOSITES

Bertie is driving over the bridge. Where is Thomas going?

The shed doors are open and James is coming out.

James has gone to bed. Are the doors open or shut?

Toby is in the big, wide shed.

Now he is going into the narrow tunnel.

Harold the Helicopter flies up in the sky.

Henry travels down below on his rails.

Gordon is a big engine.

Is Percy big or little?

under

down

shut

narrow

little

New Year's Day

Mother's Day

Valentine's Day

Easter

vacation

SPECIAL DAYS

It's the first day of the year. Thomas is having a party. What colors are the balloons?

On Mother's Day, Toby takes children to town to buy flowers.

On Valentine's Day, Thomas's driver sends his wife a card with his love.

On Easter, Sir Topham gives eggs to the children.

In the summer, people go to the seaside for their vacation.

It's Thomas's birthday. How many cards did he get?

James is taking some children to school. What are they carrying?

On Halloween, children dress up and go trick-or-treating.

It's carnival day. What colors are the girls in the band wearing?

It's Christmas. Who will bring presents for the engines?

birthday

school day

Halloween

carnival

Christmas